PHOEBE
Goes Wild

PHOEBE
Goes Wild

a. k. winter

Otterbourne press

Phoebe Goes Wild by A K Winter
Published by Otterbourne Press

© A K Winter 2021

All illustrations by
Jo Anne Davies at Artful Doodlers -
© A K Winter

Cover design and typesetting by Liz Benjamin
www.little-silver.net

ISBN: 978-1-91-630452-9

I . . . .

am officially one of
Phoebe's Friends!

Scroggins' Scrapyard

Acorn Cottage
(Phoebe's Home)

Pear Tree
Park

The
Shepherd's
Cottage

Chudleigh Hall

Church

Golf Course

The
Snorings

Wildlife Park

Soggy Wallop

Contents

Chapter One. p1

Chapter Two p13

Chapter Three. p25

Chapter Four p33

Chapter Five. p45

Chapter Six. p55

Chapter Seven p73

Chapter 1

It was a lovely sunny morning as Phoebe lay on the sofa next to her daddy. He was reading the newspaper and enjoying his first cup of tea of the day. She rested her chin on his lap and looked at the pages.

Phoebe wasn't very good at reading yet, but she liked to look at the pictures. Mostly they were of people, but when he turned the next page, she saw a picture of some strange animals. They were brown and white with very long legs and even longer necks.

"Well, look at that Phoebe," said her daddy. "They've just had a baby giraffe born at Chudleigh Wildlife Park."

A baby jurruff?

Phoebe had never seen a giraffe but guessed it must be the funny looking animal in the picture.

She had heard of the wildlife park though. Her friend Warren had told her about it when he was getting her unstuck from her garden fence. He might have mentioned juruffs too.

She had an idea. *Warren knows where the park is. I'll go and ask him the way, and then I can go and see the jurruffs.*

She licked her daddy's hand and climbed down from the sofa.

She had the whole day ahead of her. If it wasn't too far, she might be able to get there and back before tea-time.

She stepped out through her new door flap and walked to the bottom of the garden. Behind the bushes was the fence with a loose panel. She pushed her head through the hole, then climbed through to the field on the other side. She started to make her way along the edge of the field.

"Warren?" she called.

The long grass rustled and out hopped a grey rabbit.

"Hello Phoebe. Where are you off to today?"

"I want to go to see the jurruffs at Chugley Park. Can you tell me how to get there?"

"What are jurruffs?"

"I'm not zackly sure, but they have really, really long necks and they're as tall as those trees."

"Aah, you mean the giraffes. They definitely have those at Chudleigh Park. It's not all that far. You just need to go to the bottom of the field, cross the stream and…"

Warren stopped, noticing the puzzled little frown on Phoebe's face. "I'll come with you and show you the way. Come on."

Warren hopped away and Phoebe fell into step beside him.

The two friends made their way along the edge of the field and down towards the stream. It wasn't very deep and Warren showed Phoebe how to jump from one rock to another.

She was quite relieved that she hadn't had to swim. She wasn't sure how good she would be at swimming.

They were now on a little path that ran along the edge of the stream.

"That way takes you Chudleigh Hall," said Warren, pointing to the right. He hopped off to the left. "And this way leads to the Wildlife Park."

Phoebe shook her paws dry and then trotted along with him. They followed the path around the hill and through a little wood. When they came out from the trees Phoebe could see a tall fence.

"This is it," said Warren. "The people have to go in through a big gate on the other side of the park, but we can go in here."

Phoebe followed Warren as he lead her up to the fence. It wasn't like the fence at the end of her garden. This one was very high but the gaps in it were quite wide. Wide enough for a little dog and a rabbit to hop through easily.

They pushed through some bushes and emerged onto a big, winding path.

"These paths lead you all the way around the park," explained Warren. "There are lots of signs to show you the way."

Phoebe's worried look had returned. "I'm not very good at reading Warren."

"You don't need to be able to read them," he reassured her. "You

can just look at the pictures. He
hopped over to a tall pole.

"See Phoebe? These poles show you pictures of the animals and point to where they are. Do you think you'll be OK with those?"

"Yes thank you Warren. I can do pictures," she replied confidently.

"OK. Now, do you remember the way home?"

"I go through the fence, through the wood and down the path. Then over the stream and then around the field until I get to my garden."

"That's it. Just remember to keep the hill on your left until you reach the stream. Then keep the field on your left until you reach your garden. I think I'll just go and see my friends the beavers before I go back. Bye Phoebe. Have fun."

"Bye Warren," Phoebe called after him as he hopped along the path and around the corner.

Now, where are the jurruffs?

She studied the pictures on the pole but she couldn't see anything that looked like a giraffe. With no clues to go on, she picked the first path and set off.

Chapter 2

SPLISH!

What's that? SPLOSH!

There it is again.

SPLASH!

It sounds like my bath!

"Chirrup, chirrup," "hee, hee"

Excitedly, Phoebe hurried to the end of the path. The noises were coming from an enclosure with a huge pool surrounded by rocks.

The animals in there looked very odd to Phoebe. They were black and white, with black eyes and

orange beaks. They were standing up on their back legs and flapping their little arms.

What are they?

She didn't think they were birds because they didn't seem to have wings. Anyway, they weren't

flying, they were doing a funny, wobbly walk.

At that moment, two of them jumped off the rocks and plunged into the water.

Once they were in the water they darted around like fish. They were so fast!

Phoebe was puzzled. *What can they be?* She edged nearer to the fence to get a closer look.

"Hello," called a voice. Phoebe jumped back, startled. She saw one of the funny-looking animals standing on a rock just below her.

"Hello, what kind of animals are you?"

"We're penguins," he replied. "Haven't you seen a penguin before?"

"No, I haven't. Do you like being a peng gwin?"

"Yes, I suppose so. But I don't know what it's like not to be a penguin. I've never been anything else."

"I think I'd like to be a peng gwin," Phoebe replied.

"Well, why don't you come and have a go?"

"Ooh, yes please."

Phoebe squeezed under the fence and into the enclosure.

"How did you learn to swim?" she asked.

"Our mummies and daddies taught us when we were very small.

Haven't your mummy and daddy taught you to swim?"

"No. They're teaching me lots of things, but they haven't taught me to swim yet."

"Well, I suppose it's a bit like running, only you do it under the water. Just jump in and try."

Phoebe looked at all the penguins who were darting about in the water. It looked an awful lot deeper than the stream, and she hesitated for a moment.

They do make it look very easy though, she thought. *I'm sure I can do that.*

Taking a deep breath, she ran to the edge of the pool and jumped in.

SPLASH!

Her head went under the water and it filled her ears.

She struggled to the surface, coughing and spluttering. She paddled as hard as she could, but her paws were only little.

Try as she might, she couldn't keep up with the penguins. They were diving and dashing around her. All she could do was try to keep her head above water. This was not nearly so much fun as it had looked.

Desperately, she paddled towards the edge of the pool. She lunged for the rocks and clung on.

Her paws were slipping as she struggled to pull herself up.

THWUMP!

The penguin had given her a big shove from behind.

She flew through the air and landed on the top of the rock.

He jumped out of the pool and landed next to her.

"Still think you'd rather be a penguin?" he asked.

Phoebe shook herself dry and sneezed the water out of her nose.

"No, I don't think so," she replied, coughing. "I don't like swimming as much as I thought I would."

"Perhaps you're better off being a dog than a penguin?"

"Yes, praps I am," she agreed.

She clambered back through the fence and gave herself another shake. Then she set off again down the path.

Chapter 3

The next enclosure was much bigger. It had a high, wire fence and a wire roof. There was no water in it but there were lots of tall poles and trees.

A tyre on a rope hung from one of the trees. Swinging on the tyre was a hairy animal. It had big brown eyes and long arms. It seemed to be having great fun, swinging to-and-fro on the tyre.

That looks fun!

"Excuse me," Phoebe called. "What sort of animal are you?"

"I'm a chimpanzee," he replied as he swung around.

"I think I might like being a chin pansy. Could I have a go on your tyre?" she asked.

"Yes, if you like. There's a small gap in the fence over there."

Phoebe went over to the gap he had pointed to and squeezed herself through. She trotted over to him and looked up with dismay. The tyre was very high up.

"I can't reach."

"Don't worry, I'll come and get you," he said, jumping down. He scooped her up in his hairy arms.

"There you go," he said, plonking her onto the tyre.

"ooo..OO..OER!"

Phoebe tried to hold on, but her paws weren't really made for this. The chimp climbed up next to her and the tyre started to spin.

Phoebe wobbled and was about to topple off when he caught her.

"Hang on to my back," he instructed, and Phoebe did as she was told.

Then he started to swing on the tyre. It rocked backwards and forwards, then he spun it round and round. He shuffled up the rope and dangled by one arm.

Phoebe was feeling very dizzy and closed her eyes. She opened them just at the wrong moment. With one huge swing, the chimp had launched himself into the air.

They were flying!

Ooh, I don't like this! thought Phoebe, clamping her eyes shut again and hanging on tightly.

This definitely wasn't as much fun as it had looked!

"oof!"

she gasped as the chimp caught hold of another rope.

"Do you think I could get down now?" The funny feeling in her head had spread to her tummy.

The chimp laughed and climbed down, putting her safely on the ground.

"How did you learn to climb like that?" she asked, still feeling very wobbly and rather dizzy.

"My parents taught me when I was a baby," he replied. "Didn't yours teach you?"

"No. I'm dopted so I have a new mummy and daddy. They're teaching me lots of things, but they haven't taught me climbing yet. In any case, I'm not sure I like it after all."

"Perhaps you're better off being a dog than a chimp?" he said.

"Yes, praps I am," she replied as she clambered back out, on rather wobbly legs!

Chapter 4

Phoebe carried on along the path. Ahead of her was another enclosure with trees in it.

Maybe it's more chin pansies, she thought. *If it is, I will keep walking!*

She got closer and closer but couldn't see anything. She pushed her nose right up to the fence and stared at the trees, looking for chimps.

"RRROOARR!"

CRASH!

A bellowing, yellow beast lunged
at the fence. Phoebe was bowled
over by a blast of hot air from its
gaping mouth. She rolled over and
over down the path.

When she came to a stop, she warily opened her eyes. The beast was furiously throwing itself at the fence!

"GRRR... OWW... WWWLL!"

Well, whatever that animal is, I don't want to be one. In any case, I'm not asking to go in there!

She picked herself up and shook the dust from her coat. The angry animal's hot breath had given her a blow dry!

She saw she was under a sign-post. She didn't know the word, but she recognised the picture.

It's a jurruff!

Excitedly, she took off in the direction of the sign.

She went over a little bridge and past a long, high fence. Then she turned a corner and there they were. They were brown and white, and had very long legs and even longer necks.

One of animals was ambling over towards her.

"Hello," called Phoebe. "Are you a jurruff?"

"Yes, I am," she replied.

"I thought so. I saw a picture of your baby in the paper."

"Oh yes, she's famous now. She finds all the attention quite tiring though. She's having a sleep at the moment."

Phoebe was confused. *Why is she calling her Fay Mouse? She's a jurruff, not a mouse.*

"Sorry she's not here to say hello. Would you like to come in though?"

"Ooh, yes please."

Phoebe stepped through the fence. She couldn't believe how tall the giraffe was.

Phoebe's head only just reached her ankle!

"It must be lovely being so tall," she said. "I think I'd like to be a jurruff. You must be able to see everything from up there."

"Well, you can come up and have a look if you like." She bent down and Phoebe scrambled up onto her head.

Ooh, this is fun! Phoebe could see right over the tops of all the enclosures. She could see the scary animal with the big roar ("he's a lion," the giraffe informed her), the chimps swinging in their trees and the penguins swimming in their pool. She could see for miles!

"What do you do up here?" she asked.

"Most of the time we eat."

"Eat what?"

"Leaves."

"Leaves? That doesn't sound very nice."

"Well, try some for yourself."

With that she walked slowly over to a tree where the other giraffes were nibbling on the leaves. Phoebe leaned forward and took a bite of one of the leaves.

"uuuuugh!"

"Puh!"

She spat it out!

"Haven't you eaten leaves before?"

"No, my mummy gives me food in a bowl, and it tastes much nicer than that."

"Well then, perhaps you are more suited to being a dog than a giraffe?"

"Yes, praps I am," agreed Phoebe.

The giraffe walked back to the fence and lowered her head right down to the ground. Phoebe jumped off and onto the path.

"Come back another time and you can meet our baby."

"Yes, thank you, I will. I'd like to meet Fay," she called, as she trotted away.

"Who's Fay?" called the puzzled giraffe, but Phoebe didn't hear.

Chapter 5

As Phoebe was deciding where to go next, she heard the strangest noises.

"uugh, uugh, UOofFF
uugh, uugh, UOofFF"

SPLOSH!

The sounds seemed to be coming from around the corner, so Phoebe made her way towards them.

When she turned the corner, she saw a big pond full of muddy water. At first, she thought there was nothing in there. Then she saw the water rippling. Feeling curious, she shuffled under the fence and edged nearer.

Suddenly, the whole pond seemed to be moving. A bulky, grey shape appeared from under the water.

"woaaAARRR"

The roar came from the most enormous mouth Phoebe had ever seen!

The beast clambered out of the pond and she saw that it had a huge body too, and legs as wide as tree trunks!

She was suddenly very scared and wished she hadn't got so close.

At that moment it turned towards her. The ground shuddered with every step it took. Its eyes met hers and she trembled under its stare.

"WHO ARE YOU?"

"I'm Phoebe" she replied in a very wobbly voice.

It was still walking towards her and with every step it seemed to get three times as big. It came to a stop right in front of her and she cowered underneath its gigantic shadow.

"What are you doing in my enclosure?" he roared.

"I was just curos," she answered nervously. "I wanted to see what kind of animal you are."

"And what kind of animal am I then?"

"I'm not zackly sure. Are you an ellyfant?"

At this, his huge mouth opened really wide and Phoebe was sure he was going to eat her up!

"An elephant?" he laughed. "Why do you think I am an elephant?"

"Well, because I think they are very big and grey, like you," explained Phoebe.

"Well, you're right, they are big and grey. But they have much

bigger ears than me. They have a trunk too, and I don't."

"You mean a suitcase?"

"No, not a suitcase," he chortled. "It's like a very long nose," he explained. "But elephants can pick up things with it too."

"That sounds very clever," said Phoebe. "But if you're not an elly-fant, what are you?"

"I'm a hippopotamus."

"A hippomopatus?"

"A hippopotamus."

"Hipperopatus?"

"No, hippopotamus"

This was a very long word for a little dog who didn't know many words! Phoebe tried again.

"Hipper hopper mouse?"

"No, hipp…look, just say 'hippo', it's much easier."

"What do you do all day, hippo?"

"Mostly I wallow in mud. That's my favourite thing to do."

Phoebe thought back to her first home and the muddy garden where she'd been tied up. She used to try to keep out of the mud. She was sure she hadn't wallowed in it, even though she wasn't sure what wallow meant.

"I don't like mud at all," she said. "I don't think I would like to be a hippo."

"No? Well, it's not for everyone," he said. "Anyway, if you have no more questions, I have some wallowing to be getting on with. Sure you don't want to give it a try?"

"No thank you," said Phoebe. "I really won't like wallowing."

"Please yourself," he said. "And take care. You shouldn't be climbing into enclosures. Some of the animals are very dangerous. I normally am, but you've caught me on a good day."

"I will," said Phoebe, as she climbed back out. Behind her she heard a big splosh and the sounds of a hippo wallowing!

She wondered what to do next. *Maybe there are ellyfants here. I might see if I can find them. I'd better not climb in any more closures though.*

She set off down the path again.

Chapter 6

Phoebe was looking for some signs with pictures on them when she heard a familiar sound. It was children laughing. Phoebe liked children very much.

Praps I can play with them, she thought. And with a spring in her step, she made her way towards the sound.

The path was full of twists and turns, but the sound was getting nearer.

Then around the corner she saw a big sign:

She was staring at the letters, wondering what they said, when—

Plop!

A big raindrop landed on her back.

She looked up at the sky but it was bright blue. There were no rainclouds in sight.

That's odd.

She looked back at the sign and—

SPLAT!

A huge raindrop hit her on the back of the head. She looked up at the sky again, but no, there were definitely no clouds.

"Hee, hee, hee!"

She spun around to where the noise had come from.

Behind a log fence, three very tall sheep with long necks were huddled together, giggling.

What are they laughing at?

She turned away and quickly turned back. As she did—

something wet smacked her straight between the eyes!

"OW!"

She blinked hard.

"Ooops!"

"Hee, hee, hee!"

Phoebe was very cross. She didn't very often get cross, but this was one of those times when cross was the only thing to be.

She marched over to the fence. "Who did that?"

The sheep looked…sheepish!

They looked at the ground, and each other, but not at Phoebe.

She scrambled up the logs to the top of the fence. Now she was almost as tall as them.

They backed away from the fence, trying not to look guilty. It wasn't working. They were the guiltiest looking sheep Phoebe had ever seen (actually, she'd never seen any sheep before. Still, she felt fairly sure that this is what guilty sheep would look like)!

"I said, who did that?"

"Did what?"

"Spitting."

"Not me."

"Nor me."

"Well I know it was one of you. You're setting a very bad zample. The children will think if it's ok for sheep, it's ok for them, won't they?"

One of the sheep gingerly ambled over towards her.

"Sorry. It was just a bit of fun. We didn't mean any harm. I'm an alpaca by the way."

"Well, Al Packer, I don't care what your name is. You shouldn't do it."

"I know. It's just…you've no idea how bored we get, standing here all day."

Phoebe knew what it was like to be bored. In her first home, she used to spend all her days tied up. She'd had nothing to do and no one to play with.

"You're not tied up though. You have all this lovely space to play in. You have children coming to see you too."

"The children don't spend much time with us. They prefer the animals they can pick up, or feed, or ride."

"Can't they ride you? You look big enough."

"No, we don't like having things on our backs."

"Oh, I see. Well, why not give them rides in a cart then? (Phoebe had seen a picture of one in Daddy's paper). You could pull a cart, couldn't you?"

"I've never thought about it. But now you mention it, I suppose we could. I'll see what the others think, but it sounds fun to me. Sorry again about the spitting."

"It's ok," replied Phoebe, gracefully. "But I hope you get your cart so you won't be bored anymore. Otherwise, I'll need a raincoat if I come back!"

"Do come again. I promise we won't spit at you next time!"

Phoebe laughed. She wasn't cross any more.

"Ok, I will. Bye Al."

"Who's Al?" asked the alpaca, but Phoebe didn't hear.

So a rather confused alpaca bounded off to tell his friends the exciting new plan!

Now, what's through here? wondered Phoebe, as she walked past the sign that she couldn't read. She could still hear children laughing, so she followed the sound.

There were little fields on each side of the path, surrounded by a wooden fence. Some children were climbing on the fence, stroking an animal on the other side.

As she got closer she could see it looked like a horse, but it had a longer coat and much bigger ears.

Phoebe stood in front of the fence.

"Hello, are you a horse?" she asked.

"No, I'm a donkey."

"What's the difference?"

"I have a longer coat and much bigger ears."

I knew that! thought Phoebe, feeling very pleased with herself. She liked it when she knew things. "I'd really like to be petted by the

children. Do you think I could come in with you?"

"Yes, if you like."

Phoebe clambered through the fence and into the paddock with the donkey.

She stood next to it and the children started to pat and stroke her too.

This is lovely, she thought, as they rubbed her ears and tickled her chin.

"Is this what you do all day, stand here being stroked by children? It's really nice."

"Well almost. I have another job to do as well."

"What's that?"

As the donkey was about to reply a man opened a gate in the fence. He had something like Phoebe's lead in one hand, and a big brown thing over his arm. He stood next to the donkey and put the thing on her back. It looked like a seat of some kind. Then he buckled the lead around her head.

A little boy, climbed through the fence and stood by the donkey. The man lifted him onto her back and led the donkey away.

They walked slowly at first, and the boy smiled and waved at his friends. Then the man started

running, and the donkey trotted along beside him. The little boy dug his heels into her and laughed as he bounced up and down.

Well, that doesn't look fun at all!

Phoebe loved children but she knew she couldn't carry one on her back. After all, she was only little. *And all that kicking!*

She climbed back through the fence.

I don't actually think I'd like to be a donkey.

Phoebe thought it was time she went home. It must be nearly tea-time and her mummy would wonder where she was.

She followed the path, hoping it would lead her to the way out. The trouble was, she couldn't remember where she had come in! Warren had led her through the fence, but where was that? She remembered how to do the bit beyond the fence—

through the wood ....

... down the path ...

... across the stream ...

... around the field.

But how was she to find the fence? She hadn't thought of that.

I know. If I go to all the animals I saw, but backwards, I should end up where I started.

It seemed like a fine plan. All she had to do was find them.

chapter 7

Phoebe was standing in front of a signpost, trying to work out which way to go.

The last animal I saw before the donkey and the funny sheep was the hopper mouse.

She looked for a picture of a hippo on the sign.

That looks like one, she thought, and she started off in the direction of the arrow.

After Phoebe had walked a little way along the path, she heard a familiar sound.

splosh ... slosh

That sounds like the hopper mouse. So, I follow the path round this closure and then go towards the jurruffs.

As she walked past the hippo enclosure, there was a yellow flash—

b o i n g

A bright ball bounced across the path in front of her.

"Excuse me!"

Phoebe looked around to see
where the voice was coming from.

"Over here!"

A grey head was poking over
some rocks in the enclosure, but it
wasn't the hippo.

"Hello," she replied. "What are you doing in the hopper mouse's home?"

"What's a hopper mouse?"

"The big, grey animal that likes mud and doesn't have a suitcase."

"Oh, you mean the hippo! This isn't his home, it's ours. We're seals."

"Oh." Phoebe was confused. *That's odd, I was sure I was going the right way.*

"Could you pass our ball back please?"

"OK"

Phoebe picked up the ball in her mouth, which wasn't easy. It was quite a big ball and she only had little mouth!

"Wha ga aa ya aing?"

"Sorry?"

She tried again.

"Waa gai aoo ayng?"

"I can't make out what you're saying. Pass me the ball and then try."

Phoebe stood by the fence and flung the ball upwards, as hard as she could.

The seal leaned forward, bounced the ball on its nose and headed it back into the pond.

"Wow, that was clever!"

"What were you trying to say before?"

"I said, what game are you playing?"

"Water polo."

"What's that?"

"It's polo, but in water."

Phoebe was none-the-wiser. She'd never heard of polo.

"Do you want to try it?"

"No thank you. I'm not very good in water."

"All right."

"honk"   "HONK"

"It sounds as though I'm wanted. I'd better get back to the game. Thanks for the ball."

"Can you tell me the way to the jurruffs?"

"Jurruffs?"

"Yes, they're really tall with long necks."

"Oh, you mean the giraffes?"

"Yes, the jurruffs. Do you know where they are?"

"Over there," he replied, pointing across the pond with his flipper. "On the far side of that field," he called, as he somersaulted into the water.

Gosh. It looks much further than I remember, thought Phoebe. *I'd better hurry.*

She scampered down the path towards the field.

She hadn't got very far when—

c r a c k !

What was that?

Then a shout came from behind some trees—

"Timber!"

Phoebe stared over at the trees.

THWUMP!

The ground shuddered beneath Phoebe's feet. She went over to the fence by the trees and pushed her nose through the wire. A tree was lying on the ground. A group of brown, furry animals were gnawing at the branches.

Drrrr   Drrrr

One by one the branches fell off, until nothing was left but the trunk. Then they all pushed and pulled it.

"Hmmmph"

"uuurgh"

Bit by bit, they dragged it down to the edge of their pond.

Phoebe was baffled.

"What are you doing?" she called to the nearest animal.

"We're making a dam," she called back.

"What's a dam?"

"It holds back the water."

"Why do you want to do that?"

"To make it deeper."

"Why do you want it deeper?"

"So we can build an entrance to our home that predators can't get in."

"What are predtas?"

"Animals that would hurt us."

"Are there any in your closure?"

"Well, no but—"

"So why do you need to keep safe from them?"

The animal frowned as she thought about that.

"Well…it's just what beavers do."

"Beavers?" *Weren't they the friends that Warren was coming to see?*

"Do you know my friend Warren?"

"Warren? Yes, he was here a little while ago. You must be Phoebe."

"Yes, I am."

"He said you were coming to see the giraffes. Did you find them?"

"I did. And I found peng gwins, and chin pansies, and a hopper potter mouse."

The beaver looked puzzled.

"Oh, and a naughty sheep called Al Packer!"

Now the beaver was really confused!

"I'm trying to get back to the jurruffs so I can find my way out. Do you know where they are?"

"Yes. But I know where Warren comes in. There's a shorter way. Can you get over the fence?"

Phoebe looked up. "I don't think so. It's too high."

"Just a minute." The beaver scuttled away and returned, dragging a branch. She stood it against the fence and then pushed it over the top. It fell over the other side and made a ramp.

"There, Phoebe. Try that."

She climbed up onto the log. "Ooh!"

It wobbled and she almost fell off. But she steadied herself and carefully made her way to the top.

Then she jumped down and they
walked over to the pond.

"Hey everyone, this is Phoebe. She needs to get across the pond. Help me take her over on the log."

The other beavers barked and grunted to each other. They pushed the log into the water and held it still for her.

"Hop on."

Phoebe stepped onto the log and wobbled as it rocked in the water.

"Oo..ooo..ooh!"

She struggled to keep her balance.

"Hold on Phoebe."

She steadied herself and the beavers pushed off.

They flapped their flat tails, and Phoebe and the tree glided through the water. The log swayed and rolled as they pushed it across the lake. She clung on.

When they reached the far side the beavers gave the log a final push.

BOOF!

It jammed into the mud.

Phoebe flew through the air and landed face first in the mud!

Thwump!

"Oops, sorry Phoebe!"

She lifted her head and snorted the mud from her nose!

"pfff"

"I'm ok."

She looked around, but nothing looked familiar.

"This doesn't look like the place I came in. Where do I go?"

"You need to get across the next enclosure. Our friends will take you the rest of the way. Follow us."

Two of the beavers clambered out of the lake and led Phoebe to the next fence.

"Anyone there?" they called.

Boing

boing

boing

Two reddish-coloured animals bounced up to the fence.

"G'day. What can we do for ya?"

Phoebe was staring at two of the strangest creatures she had ever seen.

They had small, long heads
with pointy ears. Their front legs

were very short, and they sat up on huge back legs.

They seemed to be balancing on thick, long tails.

"What are they?" Phoebe whispered.

"They're kangaroos, from Australia."

"Oh, I see."

Phoebe didn't really see. She'd never heard of kang groos and she didn't know where Straylya was.

The beavers explained the problem to the kangaroos.

"No worries. Hop over here little mate."

Phoebe tried to hop but it wasn't something she had done before.

skip ... skip ...

ooof!

Her legs got in a tangle and she fell into the mud again!

"He doesn't really mean you have to hop Phoebe," explained the beaver as she helped her up.

"Oh, good. But I still have to get over that," she sighed, looking at the fence.

"I've an idea," said the beaver. "Stand on my tail."

Phoebe did as she was told, with no idea why.

The other beaver took hold of the end of the tail.

"Ready Phoebe?" he asked.

"Ready for wha—?"

THWACK!

Whooooosh!

Phoebe had no time to finish the question. She'd been catapulted into the air!

"Aaaaargh!!"

She flew over the fence and suddenly, everything went dark. "Wha—? Where am I?"

She was upside down and her head seemed to be stuck. It felt like she was in some kind of furry bag.

She wriggled her feet and fell right inside the bag!

"Ooogh ... oourf"

She wiggled around inside the bag until she was the right way up. Then she poked her head out.

"Ooh!" She was in a pocket on the kangaroo's tummy!

"G'day Feebs. Alright in there?"

"Yes, it's very comfy thank you," she replied.

"Bonzer. Right, let's go."

Boing   boing

BOING

The kangaroo set off across the enclosure.

Phoebe leaned out of the pouch, stretched her front legs out wide, and the wind whipped through her fur.

"Wheeeeeeeee!"

I wonder if this is what it feels like to be on a boat?

She was having such fun she didn't want it to end. But all too soon they had reached the fence on the far side.

"There ya go Feebs. That's where you came into the park."

Phoebe clambered out of the pouch and jumped down to the ground.

"I just need to get over your fence first."

"No probs."

She realised what was coming only a moment before it happened!

THWACK!

Not again!

A kick from one of the kangaroo's big feet had sent her flying into the air!

"Aaaaargh!!"

Thwump!

"Oof!"

She landed in a heap on the other side of the fence. She picked herself up and dusted herself off.

"Thank you very much for the ride," she said politely (after all, it had been great fun up until she'd been kicked over the fence)!

"Anytime," called the kangaroo as she hopped back to join her friends.

GRRR... URR... OWWLL

The rumbling in her tummy reminded Phoebe it was getting near her teatime.

She went over to the big fence and squeezed herself through.

Now, what were Warren's drecshuns?...

Through the wood
Down the path
Across the stream
Around the field

Phoebe made her way through the wood. Then she followed the path to the stream and hopped across the rocks. She trotted around the edge of the field until she came to the loose part of her garden fence. She climbed through, then skipped down the path and in through her dog flap in the back door.

"Hello Phoebe," greeted her mummy as she walked in. "Have you had a nice time in the garden? You must be ready for your tea." She put a bowl of tasty fish and vegetables down for her.

I do feel very hungry after all my ventures.

And as she tucked in, she thought of the animals she had met. *They were all very nice, except that angry lion,*

but I wouldn't want to be a Peng Gwin

I don't like swimming,

or a Chin Pansy

I don't like climbing,

or a Jurruff

I don't like leaves,

or a Hipper Hopper Mouse

I don't like mud,

or a Donkey

I couldn't carry children.

I did have fun being a Kang Groo for a while

but my home is much comfier than their closure, and I have my own door.

No, of all the animals in the world, she realised she didn't want to be anyone else.

She was very happy just as she was - a little dog named Phoebe!

Phoebe

If you enjoyed reading my book
it would mean so much to me
if you could take a moment to
leave a review on Amazon.

Feedback is so very important
and is hugely appreciated.

Thank you!

Look out for these other
Phoebe and Friends adventures ...

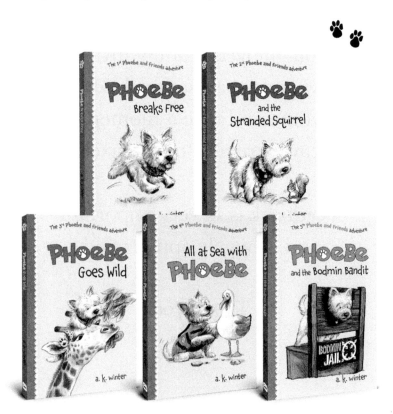

... and keep up-to-date with all the latest news on Phoebe and Friends books by visiting

akwinter.co.uk

Printed in Great Britain
by Amazon

79244846R10079